NO ONE
LIKES A
FART

For Sonny and Hamish,
my beloved tootmonsters—Zoë

For Jess, whose support
has meant the world to me—Adam

W

PENGUIN WORKSHOP
An Imprint of Penguin Random House LLC, New York

Text copyright © 2017 by Zoë Foster Blake. Illustrations copyright © 2017 by Adam Nickel. All rights reserved. First published in Australia in 2017 by Viking, an imprint of Penguin Random House Australia. Published in the United States in 2020 by Penguin Workshop, an imprint of Penguin Random House LLC, New York. PENGUIN and PENGUIN WORKSHOP are trademarks of Penguin Books Ltd, and the W colophon is a registered trademark of Penguin Random House LLC. Printed in the USA.

Visit us online at www.penguinrandomhouse.com.

Library of Congress Control Number: 2019945143

ISBN 9781524791896   10 9 8 7 6 5

NO ONE LIKES A FART

BY ZOË FOSTER BLAKE • ILLUSTRATED BY ADAM NICKEL

Penguin Workshop

Fart slipped out silently, invisibly,
when no one was paying attention.

Fart was so excited to see the big, big world and make some very best friends.

Where would he even begin?

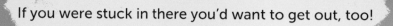

If you were stuck in there you'd want to get out, too!

Oh dear, Fart thought.
A gross smell doesn't seem very good.
I should probably go.

Fart floated off through the house. He peeked through a door and saw a boy and a roly-poly brown dog having fun.

These will be my first very best friends.

He glided over to the boy, smiling widely.

The boy sniffed. He sniffed again.
He scrunched up his face.

He looked at the dog.

What a very bad dog, thought Fart.

The boy turned a fan on. Fart was whooshed and swooshed right out the window!

Probably not a bad thing, thought Fart, once he stopped spinning. They seemed to be dealing with some kind of awful smell in that house.

Fart sailed through the warm afternoon air,
enjoying the sweet fragrances nearby.

What a beautiful world it was!
How lucky he felt to have arrived!

Life was really wonderful.

Fart gleefully whistled his way down the street.
He saw a mother pushing a stroller.

A baby! thought Fart.
Could this *be my first very best friend?*

Suddenly the mother jogged off,
sending Fart out of the stroller in a swirl.

Never mind, thought Fart.
The world is full of friends!

Fart sailed on until he reached a big, busy road.
It smelled like car exhaust and fishy cooking oil and smog.

What paradise, he thought as a noisy blue bus pulled up.

Bus! thought Fart happily.
What could be more fun than riding on a bus, seeing the world, and making some very best friends?

But before he could get on,
the bus zoomed off!

Fart waited at the bus stop with a wrinkled, crinkled old man and two girls chewing gum.

They didn't seem as happy as they should be, considering there was a bus ride ahead.

An air biscuit sounds delicious, thought Fart.

But the old man didn't seem to think so.

When the next bus arrived, Fart rushed on
as soon as the doors opened.

Three boys were laughing loudly and having
a really best-friend time.

Bro! Did you let one rip? That's *gross* . . .
You don't fart on the bus!

Fart's heart broke into big, medium, and small pieces.

It was HIM.

He was the horrible, terrible smell.

He was embarrassing and disgusting.

He would never, ever find a very best friend.

Fart wafted off the bus at the next stop.
He floated toward a little cafe.

These people look happy, Fart thought
as he pushed his face against the glass.

Surely just one of them would be his friend?

Fart slipped under the door.

Fart's sweet, hopeful little heart sank.

They thought he was repulsive. They didn't want
to be his friend, either. No one did.

I give up, thought Fart.
*I'm kind and friendly, and I'd make a wonderful very
best friend, but no one will give me a chance.*

Fart slipped out a window and into a dark, grimy alley.
It smelled like cat pee and rotting fish guts and old shrimp . . .
But not even his favorite smells could cheer him up.

This would be his home. He couldn't disgust
anyone back here.

Suddenly, a man and woman carrying
garbage bags came outside.
An enormous roar escaped
the woman's mouth.

MMMMBUUUURRRRRP

Fart was fascinated. What *was* that?

Fart noticed a small purple cloud
hiding in the shadows, sobbing quietly.

He floated slowly over to Burp.
She smelled like onions and old
cheese and dirty socks.

She was *beautiful*.

But Burp pulled away.

Am I really that horrible?

Fart thought about all the times people had been disgusted by him.

Zoë has written lots of grown-up books, none of which mention a single fart. She is the mother of two little people and a cat with a permanently cranky face. She wants it known that despite writing this book, she still doesn't like farts, even if her husband Tooty McFluffson refuses to acknowledge this.

Fart had found a very best friend.
And she smelled gross and horrible and yucky and very disgusting.

Fart could *not* have been happier.